YOU'VE LOST YOUR MARBLES,
LiCKETY SPLiT

Written and illustrated by
Harland Williams

Copyright ©1988 by Hayes Publishing Ltd.

Second Printing, 1988

All rights reserved. No part of this book may be reproduced or transmitted
in any form or by any means, electronic or mechanical, including
photocopying and recording, or by any information storage or retrieval
system, without permission in writing from the publisher.

3312 Mainway, Burlington, Ontario L7M 1A7, Canada
2045 Niagara Falls Blvd., Unit 14, Niagara Falls, NY 14304, U.S.A.

PRINTED IN HONG KONG
0-88625-178-8

In the land of prehistory
Down dinosaur way,
Seven young monsters
Played marbles one day.

There was Jo-Jo the sure shot,
And Jeff with his flick.
It seemed each young dino
Had his own special trick.

Then up stepped a monster
With his marble kit,
A small brontosaurus
Named Lickety Split.

It was his turn to shoot,
All the others had played.
If he hit the big marble,
He'd be able to trade.

Down on one knee
Went Lickety Split.
He squinted an eye
And prayed for a hit.

Our friend was quite nervous
As he lined up his shot,
And tried to remember
All the tricks he'd been taught.

But something went wrong!
The shot flew too high.
It hit a big mammoth,
Just missing his eye.

How they hooted and howled.
Jo-Jo let out a yelp,
"Ha-Ha! Lickety's shot
Hit the old mammoth's scalp."

Lickety rose from the dust
And walked slowly toward home.
"Seems the others don't like me,
But I can't play alone."

"Ouch!" His foot hit a rock.
Lickety fell to the dirt,
And before he could check
To see if he'd been hurt...

A gravelly voice yelled,
"Hey! Can't you watch out?"
Lickety stared all around.
There was no one about.

The voice seemed to come
From a rock lying near.
"That rock just spoke,
Of that I'm quite clear."

"I hope you didn't hurt your toes,"
The rock spoke up again.
But Lickety was thinking,
Perhaps he'd found a friend.

"Please don't be scared," the boulder said,
Making an anxious plea.
"I don't get many visitors,
As you are sure to see."

Lickety looked all around him.
The desert was a lonely place.
He understood the sad, sad look
Upon the gray rock's face.

"Why, I'll be your friend, Rock.
In fact, we are much the same.
Like you, I have no friends,
At least none that I can name."

"Let's have some fun, the two of us.
Let's play at hide and seek."
"But I can't move," the rock replied.
"You'd be hiding out for weeks."

"Well, how about a game of catch
With this smooth and rounded stone?"

"That stone's a distant cousin of mine.
We'd best leave it alone."

The rock could simply not play tag,
Or jump a skipping rope.
Before too long, the two new friends
Began to give up hope.

Then it dawned on the young brontosaurus,
Under the red-hot desert sun,
How he and his boulder buddy
Could still have some laughs and good fun.

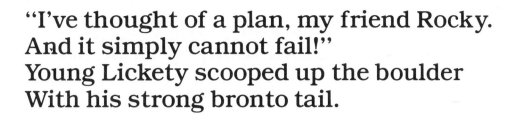

"I've thought of a plan, my friend Rocky.
And it simply cannot fail!"
Young Lickety scooped up the boulder
With his strong bronto tail.

"I will carry you to the woodland lake
Where we can swim and cool off."
Lickety marched past the old marble
game,
Holding his new friend aloft.

All dinosaurs have seen strange sights,
And have heard tales of other planets.
Not one of them had ever seen
A bronto make friends with
GRANITE!

Now that the interest in marbles was gone,
They followed Lickety Split to the lake,
And as he started into the water,
Shouted, "You're making
a DREADFUL
MISTAKE!"

The rock was happy as a clam.
Sand and water were both fine with him.
He didn't care if Lickety Split
Would sink under - or if he could swim!

Lickety Split began to notice
The rock was dragging him down.
With each stroke the rock grew heavier.
"Jump off, Rocky, or we'll drown!"

"I can't swim," the rock cried back.
"But it really doesn't matter.
I'll be just as happy down below,
So stop your foolish chatter!"

"But my legs are getting tired.
I can tell I'm going to sink!
Please, Rock friend, jump off right now!
Or I will drown, I think."

"HELP! PLEASE HELP!" yelled Lickety
Split
At the top of his water-logged throat.

His friends rushed out to his rescue,
And kept poor Lickety afloat.

W9-CXK-293

Once upon a time, a monster named Rosita lived in a tiny ,

where there was room for only a , a stove, and a bag of rice.

And in her tiny yard, Rosita had a  named Milky.

RICE

Rosita had no money and little food. What was she to do? The only thing she had to sell was her . Luckily she met a man who needed a  as company for his . "I have no money to pay for the ," said the man, "but I will trade you these magic  to plant."

"Magic ?" thought Rosita. "How can  be magic?" She planted them in the ground, then went to . When she woke up the next morning, she couldn't believe her eyes! An enormous beanstalk grew where she'd planted the .

Rosita climbed the beanstalk up, up, up into the sky. At the very top she saw a gigantic  . "Who could live in such a place?" thought Rosita. She tiptoed across a cloud, toward the .

The 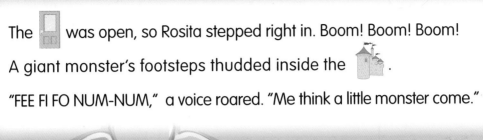 was open, so Rosita stepped right in. Boom! Boom! Boom! A giant monster's footsteps thudded inside the  .

"FEE FI FO NUM-NUM," a voice roared. "Me think a little monster come."

The giant monster was huge and the giant monster was hungry—his belly was making loud, thundery rumbles. Rosita hid behind the  . She watched as the giant monster ate a scrambled  and fell asleep at the table instead of in  .

Cluck, cluck, cluck. Rosita looked down. There sat a  on top of a huge pile of shiny golden . Rosita missed Milky and thought, "This  is too small to be a good pet for the giant, but she's just right for me." She tucked the  under her arm and tiptoed away.

Rosita climbed down, down, down the beanstalk, to her little  .
It was dinnertime, and she had worked up a giant appetite.
Luckily a golden ⬭ tastes just as delicious as a regular ⬭ .

The next morning, Rosita had an idea. She sold a golden  to buy back her 🐐 . "¡Hola!" Rosita greeted Milky. "I really missed you." "Moo!" said Milky. "Cluck!" said the 🐔 .

Seeing her  again made Rosita think. "Maybe the giant is missing his , like I missed Milky," she said. "It wasn't very nice of me to take it. I will bring it back to the ." She tucked the  under her arm and climbed up the beanstalk.

Inside the , a familiar voice roared. "FEE FI FO NUM-NUM! Me think a little monster come." The giant monster was still huge and he was still hungry. His belly was still making loud, thundery rumbles. Rosita hid behind the door again.

Rosita watched as the giant gobbled another scrambled  and fell asleep at the table instead of in . Rosita put down the  and began to tiptoe away. Then she saw a  lying on the floor.

"I love playing the !" thought Rosita. "And this one looks too small for a giant." Rosita forgot all about asking first. She picked up the  and tiptoed to the .

It turned out this  was magic! It began playing beautiful music, all by itself. The 🐔 sang along, "Cluck, cluck, cluck." All the noise woke up the giant. "FEE FI FO NUM-NUM. Me knew a little monster come!" he said. "But why you take 🎸? If you be my friend, me share 🎸 with you. And how about a scrambled ⬭?" said the giant.